There are lots of Early Reader
stories you might enjoy.

Look at the back of the book or,
for a complete list, visit
www.orionchildrensbooks.co.uk

GRANDAD'S MEDAL

GRANDAD'S MEDAL

PHIL EARLE

ILLUSTRATED BY SARAH HORNE

Orion
Children's Books

ORION CHILDREN'S BOOKS

First published in Great Britain in 2017
by Hodder and Stoughton

1 3 5 7 9 10 8 6 4 2

Text © Phil Earle, 2017
Illustrations © Sarah Horne, 2017

The moral rights of the author and illustrator have been asserted.

A CIP catalogue record for this book
is available from the British Library.

ISBN 978 1 5101 0236 1

Printed and bound in China

The paper and board used in this book are
made from wood from responsible sources.

Orion Children's Books
An imprint of
Hachette Children's Group
Part of Hodder and Stoughton
Carmelite House
50 Victoria Embankment
London EC4Y 0DZ

An Hachette UK Company
www.hachette.co.uk

www.hachettechildrens.co.uk

There are more than 695 reasons why this book is for you, Sarah Williams. — P.E.

Contents

Chapter One

Marvin LOVED adventures.

So did his grandad. He had been an explorer all his life and his house was full of objects to prove it.

Marvin loved playing there.
Everywhere he looked there was
an adventure waiting for him.

And the best thing was, he
didn't have to go on his own.
Grandad came too.

"Where shall we go today?"
Marvin would ask.

"Anywhere you want," the old
man would answer. "As long as
you take me with you."

It didn't matter that Grandad had creaky knees, or a wheezy chest.

It didn't matter that his false teeth slipped out when he got too excited.

Marvin thought he was the greatest.

WORLD'S GREATEST GRANDAD

And so they always went
exploring together.

Chapter Two

Marvin and Grandad went all around the world without ever leaving the house.

They could travel to India, or Australia, and still be home for tea.

One day, Marvin found a pair
of old skis and a huge woolly coat
in the attic.

Two minutes after he strapped
the skis to his feet, he was being
chased down a mountain by
a massive and very
hungry yeti.

The beast was scary, but Marvin never screamed.

After a long and tiring chase,
he found a half-eaten biscuit in
his pocket, which stopped the yeti
being so grumpy.

"Was I brave, Grandad?" Marvin asked when the adventure was over. Grandad took a while to answer, like he was slowly making up his mind (as well as getting his breath back).

"Quite," he answered. "Quite brave."

It wasn't the answer Marvin had hoped for.

Chapter Three

Being brave mattered to Marvin. It mattered a lot.

Most of all, it mattered that Grandad thought he was brave.

Why?

Because of an object that
hung above Grandad's fireplace.
It was the one thing Marvin
desperately wanted to play with,
and the one thing he wasn't
allowed to touch.

Grandad's medal.

It wasn't very big, a little longer than a thumb, but it shone brightly every time Marvin looked at it.

"Can I play with it today? Please?" Marvin would ask every time he visited.

"Not yet," the old man would answer.

"I earned that medal in the war, for being very, very brave. Any boy who wants to pin it on his chest has to be incredibly brave too. He has to be the bravest boy I ever met."

"I can be brave!" Marvin yelled. He picked up an old, blunt spear and spent the afternoon hunting down a terrifying tiger.

Boy, was he fearless.

So fearless that he then took
Grandad parachuting before
finishing with a day trip to Mars.

"So," he asked, after their rocket had crash-landed on the sofa, "was I brave enough today, Grandad? Was I? Was I?"

Grandad looked like he needed to sleep, but he forced his eyes open long enough to whisper, "You're getting closer. You're so very, very close, but you're not quite there yet."

And holding the boy's hand, he
fell into a deep slumber.

Chapter Four

Marvin SO wanted to play with that medal. More than ever before. But the very next day, his chances ran out.

"Grandad's too tired to play today," Mum told him. "Maybe when he's feeling stronger. Maybe tomorrow."

But tomorrow
never arrived.
And that seemed
to make Mum just
as sad as Marvin.

There were tears in her eyes
when she finally took Marvin back
to Grandad's house.

Not that Marvin felt sad. He was excited about how brave he was going to be and he ran around the house, shouting the old man's name.

But no matter how many times he called him, Grandad did not come.

"Marvin," Mum said softly as she held his hand. "Grandad isn't here any more. He's passed away. He was an old man who lived a long life. He just couldn't fit in any more adventures."

Marvin was confused. How could he not be here anymore? It wasn't fair. There were so many places they hadn't visited yet. So many adventures still to enjoy together.

But no matter how many times he begged Mum to bring Grandad back, she couldn't do it.

"We have to be strong now. We have to tidy up his house. It will be like an adventure."

Chapter Five

So Marvin did as Mum asked. Bit by bit, he helped put Grandad's things in boxes.

But Mum was finding it hard.
Tears slid down her cheeks as she
packed away the fishing rods and
helmets.

It hurt Marvin too, but objects also reminded him of their adventures.

"We caught a great white shark with that rod. Bigger than a house, it was. Huge."

Mum smiled.

Away went the tiger skin and the skis, and more tears followed.

"Grandad was a brilliant tiger,"
Marvin said, remembering, feeling
happy and sad at the same time.

It felt like he'd never go on an adventure ever again. How could he without Grandad?

Finally, after hours of packing, the house was empty.

Mum gave Marvin a hug. "You did a brilliant job. Thank you for looking after me."

As they cuddled, Marvin spotted a box sitting on the fireplace. It was small, just a little longer than a thumb.

"What's that?" he asked, picking it up.

He had no idea what was in it,
and doubted it could possibly make
him feel better. He opened it anyway,
only to be dazzled by what hid
inside.

Grandad's medal!

"Look. He left you a note."
Mum smiled, spotting a piece of
paper tucked inside the box.

Marvin stared at the wobbly
handwriting on the page. There
weren't many words, but there
were enough.

And Marvin would treasure
those words as much as the medal,
which Mum pinned proudly to his
chest.

This medal belongs to my grandson, Marvin.

The <u>bravest</u> boy I ever met.

What are you going to read next?

Don't miss
magic and adventure in the
Three Little stories.

football fun
in **Albert and the
Garden of Doom,**

or Timothy
making a special
mud pie in
Chocolate Porridge.